The Adventures of "CHUCK E. BEAVER" and Friends

SKIPPY SKUNK MAKES FRIENDS

Written by
Kiki

Illustrated by
ROBERT ELLIOTT

Published by
Montbec Inc.

Publisher
MATT ARENY

Publication Advisor
JOSE AZEVEDO

Editorial Supervisor
ETHEL SALTZMAN

Artwork Supervisor
PIERRE RENAUD

ISBN 2-89227-205-X

SKIPPY SKUNK MAKES FRIENDS

Making friends always came easily to Chuck E. He was a very likable person, one who would go out of his way to make someone feel happy and loved. Little did Chuck E. know that soon his ability to be friendly would be put to the most severe test.

It was on a Saturday morning when the Skunk family pulled up in front of their new home which was just a half mile down the road from the Beavers' house. As Mr. and Mrs. Skunk were busy unloading the moving trailer, the two young Skunk children were out looking over their new house and yard.

"Gee, Mom, Dad! Look how beautiful it is here!" shouted Skippy. "I sure hope the people here are friendlier than in our old town," he continued.

"It's going to work out just fine, Skippy," Mrs. Skunk said. "You just wait and see. You're going to make many new friends and soon you'll forget about that old place."

"Your Mom's right, Skippy!"
Mr. Skunk added. "A fresh start is just
what we needed. Those people in the
other town never took the time to get to
know us," Mr. Skunk continued. "They
just believed what others said about us."

"Why do people do that, Dad?" Skippy
asked. "We are no different than anyone
else. We just want to make friends and be
liked for who we are," he added.

"Well, son, you see sometimes people are afraid to give others a chance because they want to be like their friends." Mr. Skunk explained. "If they don't go along with their friends then they might lose them."

"But why can't everyone be friends?" Skippy questioned.

"I really don't know the answer to that, son, but it mustn't stop us from trying, right?" Mr. Skunk said with a smile.

"Right, Dad!" Skippy answered happily.

As the Skunks were continuing to unload their trailer, the Beavers' car was fast approaching with the whole family aboard.

"Say, Pop! Look over there, someone's moving into the old Foxes' house!" Chuck E. shouted.

"You're right, Chuck E!" Mr. Beaver replied. "Why don't we stop and see if they need a hand?" Mr. Beaver continued.

"Oh, yes! Let's do it!" Chuck E. yelled.

The Beavers' car pulled up in front of where the Skunks were busy unloading the rest of their trailer.

"Well, hello there!" shouted Mr. Beaver. "I'm Ben Beaver and this is my wife, Betty, and our son Chuck E. We'd all like to welcome you to our town and give you a hand if you need it."

"Why, thank you," Mr. Skunk replied happily. "We sure could use the help."

"I'm Sam Skunk and this is my wife, Sally, and over there are our two children, Skippy and Sandy," Mr. Skunk continued.

At that moment, Chuck E. ran over to where Skippy and Sandy were playing and introduced himself.

"Hi! I'm Chuck E! It sure is exciting having new people move onto our road!"

"Hi, Chuck E., my name's Skippy, and this is my sister, Sandy," Skippy replied. "It sure is nice to meet you and get such a nice welcome to our new home."

"Well, I hope we can be good friends. We live just down the road and I'm sure we'll be seeing a lot of one another," Chuck E. added.

"In fact, I know just about everyone in the area and I'd be glad to introduce you both to them," Chuck E. continued.

"That would be great, wouldn't it, Sandy?" Skippy said with a smile.

"It sure would!" Sandy agreed.

"Say, we could do it tomorrow!" Chuck E. beamed. "We're all going down to the lake for a picnic and a swim, and you could meet everyone then!"

"Wow! Sounds terrific!" Skippy shouted. "We'll ask our father and I'm sure he'll say okay!"

"Great! Then it's all set. We're going to have a really good time, just wait and see!" Chuck E. replied happily.

That night Skippy and Sandy asked
their father about joining everyone for the
picnic and he said yes.

Soon it was morning and just about
everyone was at the lake.

The Beaver and Skunk families were
just arriving and as soon as the cars were
parked, Chuck E. and Skippy rushed over
to where all of the other kids were
playing.

"Hey, everyone!" Chuck E. shouted, "I'd like you all to meet my new friend, Skippy Skunk."

"Say, Chuck E!" Chippy Chipmunk replied loudly, "what are you doing hanging around with him?"

"Yeah, Chuck E! Don't you know about his kind?" Marty Moose added. "Nobody likes them and we don't want him as a friend either!"

"What do you mean?" Chuck E. responded angrily. "What don't you like about Skippy and his family?"

"People say they're not like the rest of us and we shouldn't be their friends," Gerty Goose said.

And with that Skippy quickly turned and ran back towards the car crying.

"Now look what you've done!" Chuck E. yelled. "You've hurt his feelings badly and he didn't do anything to you except try and be your friend."

"Oh, he'll get over it, Chuck E.," Chippy said. "Come on and join us for a swim!"

"No! I'm not joining you bullies!" Chuck E. replied. "I have to go and see Skippy. He needs a friend right now."

"Well, if that's the way you want it then you're not our friend anymore. Right, gang?" Marty shouted.

"Right!" everyone agreed.

As Chuck E. turned and started towards where Skippy was sitting all alone, he thought to himself that he didn't want to lose all of his friends but he didn't want to hurt Skippy either.

Chuck E. was now torn between doing what he felt was right and wanting to be with his friends. Chuck E. didn't know what to do so he went over to see his Pop who was busy unloading the car for the picnic.

"Pop, can I ask you something important?" Chuck E. said.

"Sure, son," Mr. Beaver replied. "You know I always have time for your important questions."

"Well, Pop, you see my friends don't want Skippy to be part of our group because of what they have heard others say about the Skunks," Chuck E. explained, "and because I still want to be his friend they don't want me around either."

"I see. Well, son," Mr. Beaver responded, "let me try to explain something about some people that is not very nice. When people dislike someone for what they look like or for what others have said about them, it is called prejudice. It is the worst type of hate there is because it is all false. Sometimes people go along with this to feel part of a group, because they are scared to go against their friends and find out the truth. But you know, son, it only takes one strong person to show us the real truth."

"I'm not afraid to show those guys the real Skippy, Pop!" Chuck E. replied proudly. "I know Skippy's not a bad person and I want the others to see that too!"

"That's my boy!" Mr. Beaver said.

At that Chuck E. quickly ran over to where Skippy was sitting by himself, looking very sad.

"Hey, Skippy!" Chuck E. shouted, "let's go swimming!"

"But what about your friends, Chuck E?" Skippy replied with hesitation. "Aren't you afraid of what they might think of you?"

"No, I'm not," Chuck E. said confidently. "I'm your friend, and if they don't like that then that's too bad!"

Chuck E. and Skippy ran into the water and began playing cheerfully, in clear view of the other kids. The gang noticed this and stopped to see Chuck E. and Skippy having a great time tossing a beach ball around.

"Say, look over there, Chuck E.'s playing with that new Skunk kid!" Chippy Chipmunk shouted.

"Yeah, and he looks like he's having a lot of fun," Marty Moose added. "Maybe we were wrong about him. Maybe he's not so bad after all."

"You know, Marty might be right!"
Rodney Racoon said. "Say, why don't we
go over and join them and give the new
kid a chance."

"Yeah, let's do it!" the gang shouted.

And with that the gang rushed over to
where Chuck E. and Skippy were playing
and joined in the fun.

"Hey, Skippy, throw me the ball over
here!" Chippy shouted.

"No, Skippy, throw it over here!"
Marty said.

"How about over here, Skippy?" Gerty
yelled.

As the others were busy trying to get Skippy to play with them, Chuck E. looked over at him with a big smile on his face.

"Thanks, Chuck E., you're a real friend!" Skippy shouted.

Chuck E. smiled to himself and thought, "So are you, Skippy, so are you."

Don't judge someone

From what others may say.

Get to know them first

And it just might make your day.

Your friend,

Chuck E.